PRAISE FOR JUSTIN ARMSTRONG'S
WYOMINGS

"This is what happens when you live inside a dream not knowing if you're the dreamer or the dreamed. When you don't know if you're trying to escape or go home. When you don't know if you're human or something adjacent, if you are chasing or being chased, if your memories are disappearing or being taken. This is what happens when you lose the lover you've loved through a million lifetimes. This is what happens when you try to find her. In these lushly landscaped dreams, Justin Armstrong ushers us through a story of grieving across time and space, across countless iterations of Wyomings. These pages plot an impossible escape from inevitable history. They chronicle foiled attempts to reconcile love and loss, and through meticulous imagery, they express the precise and painful ways we experience love."

—Lena Bertone, author of *Behind This Mirror*

"A dreamy love poem spanning thousands of miles with enough darkness to keep it grounded and heartbreaking."

—Shane Jones, author of *Light Boxes*

"There is this thing called ficto-criticism and then there is Justin Armstrong's ghostworld of the High Plains where Wyoming slides next to Freud's Vienna or Kathleen Stewart's places on the side of the road as a new capital of dreams, ethnographic hauntings and recast memories."

—Allen Shelton, author of *Dreamworlds of Alabama*

"Mapping a hallucinatory journey across time, space, memory, and emotion, Justin Armstrong creates a slipstream-dream—a jigsaw puzzle of imagination and ingenuity."

—N. J. Campbell, author of *Found Audio*

"Gosh, this book is beautiful and deadly. It's a mystery like Twin Peaks is a mystery - less about solution and more about what will always remain unknowable, the strange and uncanny in the worlds we know and those we only guess at."

—Amber Sparks, author of
The Unfinished World and Other Stories

"This story is wind, and bone, and a beautiful feral haunting across a shifting geography, creating memory inside of a rendering of time, and love, and loss. This text continues to tell stories long after the last word on the page—a blood sacrifice made in a river constantly trying to find its way home. Dissolution and building of worlds, lives folded against each other, builds a language that will stay forever with the reader. *Wyomings* is a song, and the process of listening to this text is a letting go as well as a letting in, the story tugs always, toward a beginning and a reconciliation."

—Jordan Okumura, author of *Gaijin*

"There are books that are about another time, another place, or there are books from another time, another place. And then there is this book, Justin Armstong's lyrical longitundinal study, Wyomings, that choreographs and chronographs a gross of unsquared dances, surveying, section after section of gridded prose, precincts and burroughs and townships and jurisdictions and coundies and states of beforing and being and becoming and anding. Read the tender telegraphy of each piece, the quantum mechanics of spectural light. The ethereal prose can be read as elongated titles affixed to a wall of paint sample chips, scaled to define the 200 shades of white that is the space in the space below the cloud of text—gloss, eggshell, flat, flat, flat of flat."

—Michael Martone, author of
Michael Martone and *Winesburg, Indiana*

WYOMINGS

Justin Armstrong

Cover art and design by Jana Vukovic.
Prepress by sunnoutside.

ISBN-10: 1-937662-14-4
ISBN-13: 978-1-937662-14-1

Acknowledgments: Molly Gaudry for belief and anchors; Allen Shelton for fever dreams and Buffalo; Shane Jones for February; Greg Rhyno for insight and foresight; Anne Brydon for Iceland; Petra Rethmann for Moscow; Joe, Wendy, Auralea and Amber for a wilderness of love; Meaghan, Dave, Mayotte, Jon and Adam for our northern constellations; TK, JS and AP for ghoststructuralism; Brian and Lynne for guest rooms and safe harbors; Mark Rhyno for Hamilton, Ontario; Ian Brewster for white bears and islands; my Wellesley College students for joyful inspiration; Boston, Ithaca, Thunder Bay, Hamilton, Fogo Island, Grand Bruit, Reykjavik and Muli; Trout for running and thinking; and always forever, Heather Mattila for what I have been and am—you are all that is to me.

FOR
Joseph Wayne Armstrong
(1949–2013)

WYOMINGS

Bergen, Norway, 1970

It's too late. Everything changed in the valley tonight. Whenever you've been able to decode this message I hope you were able to outrun the last of the Clouds.

Did we get out of the loops? I'm not sure why 1970 was the end point. The Two were here. I saw them just before I got pulled back in.

I can't remember when it started. Seventeen years from now? A hundred? When are you reading this?

It happened so slowly. Do you remember? Or maybe you don't know yet. Time started evaporating in little pieces. Then our Doubles started slipping into the corners of our consciousness. Their eyelashes were different. Hardwired arrows instead of bird wings. They didn't move the same.

People didn't just look like the Doubles. There were two of them, a Dreamer version and us, the Firsts. About the same time the Doubles found their way into our world we started discovering openings to other times, rips like heat waves in reality. Once we were inside we didn't know how to get out. And when I lost you in some smashed-in version of North Dakota I had to go deeper to find you. All those hurricanes of years.

I might be the last. I haven't seen another First in a long time. I hope that isn't true but I think it's unlikely there are any of us left.

Most of us never saw it coming. They just melted into themselves as the Doubles devoured them at night. Those of us who could hide from our twins sought refuge in these new time slips and the cast-off places in between. Slits in the continuum coveting our blood. Hoping to find each other once we were lost, looking for clues in undead curves in the road. Hoping to catch the beginning, the point when and where that world started seeping into ours. Bandages to keep it hidden, remember? No.

Still I don't know which world belongs to them and which is the one I've traveled for longer than I know.

We watched it roll in across what was left of North Dakota. Slow like a drugged-up dream too dizzy to stand up by itself. Then it was over. We were shadows on the run.

No one knew where it started. In the beginning we missed a few seconds here and there. A clock slowed in an office in Rapid City. Glitchy delays in Gabon's phone lines. It crept in like forgetting, some sort of diseased rotten time.

We saw ourselves beyond mirror frames catching glimpses of ourselves on the edge of our vision. Flickers of people with faces almost ours. No one said anything. No one was falling apart. Until we started murdering ourselves in our sleep.

Those who hadn't yet seen ourselves—at least not in the daylight—looked for a way to hide, for an escape to Before. The Dreamers knew we could smell them. Their sweet low scent like bleach and rosewater. They knew we shouldn't be here. Back from other Befores. Some of us were still here running down the present, a wayward scratch on the eyes of the future.

Memory and the things that were real. Dreams and broken codes. Not much sense in all of these back-and-forths jumping from then to then always trying to untie ourselves from this knot of loops looking for the real Before and not these wrecked dreams of never-before that hold us at length.

We got separated outside Fargo. One of their Clouds caught us out on the highway where we stopped to sleep. My turn to watch, and in a moment I'm not there anymore. I'm here. You're gone and I'm bleeding out in some place with two suns.

The Dreamers made the Clouds in another place and brought them to our time. The Clouds helped them find the remainders. Last lives lived in half-light. They sent them through the Befores looking for us—the other versions of themselves the them-before. Our presence was too unpredictable too dangerous. We were like paper cuts to them. We couldn't smell the Clouds until they were on us—hot dust and mineral air. At that point, I'd only ever seen one other Cloud. In a dream of my father's death.

I kept this notebook as the world broke. Flaking off in narrow crystals, fragments of our splintering time. Reading over my words I find it hard to believe I wrote them—warped memories held too close to the fire.

As I write these words I wonder if they've already been written and erased somewhere else and rewritten in a dead language not yet born.

This is a document of the last year of my life. Diamond-tipped cursive looping and etching.

Translator's Note

The preceding 'introduction' and the narrative that follows form a rough translation of the only surviving written document from the Old Era. The text is taken from a book found wedged into a crevice in a rock wall on St. Matthew Island, the small islet off the West African coast, one of the many 'phantom islands' people from this time period believed to be nothing but geographic mythologies.

The original language of this document is a previously unknown pidgin situated somewhere between Old Era Newfoundland English and Late Icelandic with several instances of a puzzling language with a marginal similarity to pre-Shift Livonian. With all of these languages extinct, reassembly of the text proved rather difficult, taking a team of several linguists almost four years to complete. I was given the raw texts to organize into a narrative formed out of hundreds of loose, hastily handwritten pages and a few decaying photographs.

I have done my best, given the circumstances, and I believe this document provides valuable insight into the last several months of the Era and the dire psychological conditions many of the Remainers experienced before the Shift.

The sequence of these pieces as they are

presented here offers only a suggested, speculative reading.

The forever now,

Justin Armstrong
Lecturer in Old Era Studies,
New Worley College,
Boston, Northern America

On waves of ghosted-out grass a Wyoming rises out of the Plains with veins full of leopard blood. Other times. Forever, Wyoming burns quietly under my skin.

In another Before and in another Wyoming I bled in full view of those rotted gold suns. Trickling noiselessly through the fingers held over my heart. Blood on denim like soap bubbles.

I'm half-heartedly leafing through the book on my lap as
the white car mixes with snow and the moon as we push
at this unknown length of night. If only on this night.

Dried leaves pressed between pages and little words and tightly curled sentences. Nickel-plated memories and colors. Each page so preciously tidy with silent white spaces bounding the letters. The book is called *Seventeen*—I bought it at a flea market in Maine a few summers back. The houses up here are like eggshells lit from inside. Pinpricks in the night that show their televisions and children to the road. We drive on through towns without names. Unmappable places. This undiscovered state appears without topography. I'm sleeping with the book open against my legs and you're hypnotized by snowflake trails in the headlights. North appears in the long distance.

We drive at night past little houses and towns. Through Indian reservations and bone splinters of nothingness. There are songs on the radio but the volume is low. I think I hear Paul Simon in there somewhere. Lost between the static and the quiet just beyond the edge of the headlights.

Hidden by clothes and skin, you are dying.

In the silence, I think back to when I still lived on the island.

Stopped at the side of the road. Yellow clear light. Maybe a Cloud. I'm traveling with my nine-year son. We're stopped on our way to what feels like some kind of salvation or at least a place that reminds us more of the places we've left behind. Those worlds don't exist anymore—they're a part of another life in another time where we wore different clothes. I don't know how to get back.

Our shadows rest anxiously under a scrubby bush agitated by our stillness. My son isn't nine anymore but he was when I went into the hospital. He's twenty-something. Maybe twenty-seven, twenty-eight. I'm older and the hardship of years drew cracks on my teeth and pulled out most of my hair. I look into the afternoon and see the route that winds across North Dakota. A few trees, but settlers planted them. I'm still looking, tracing her smashed-in timelines in alphabets and blood through loops and dead clusters of years. I think we were married once.

This place is an unknown North Dakota. No roads this far out. Only miles of wheat around my legs as I step from the low wooden doorframe of another prairie fever. A world of grass calls me by name. Walking out of this Before I don't look over my shoulder. My past has already tunneled back underground. There's nothing left to remember here. I looked in cabinets. I read labels on bottles. The fractured tiles and dead cotton creases. The smooth dominos and the reddish warmth of her office. An unseen hospital among earthbound waves. Atlantis of the Dakotas. A sunken city with weird powers.

History evaporates in our wake leaving a distilled nostalgia and a few time-thickened pictures in our heads. Wyoming's hot summer roads will soon dry up the once pregnant rivers of our little colony. My son wonders why we're here a lot less than I do. He is content now.

I see through the empty High Plains houses across the lake of light brown grass, and when I close my eyes the Pacific and all of its little island nations. Old Era landmasses. Last night, standing at a gas pump outside Bowman I heard you calling me in the wind.

Back in the car we keep driving through this milky gauze of another infected season. The High Plains open wider renaming us across their open-range faces. We talk about times before, before she was dead and when the world was made out of shinier ornaments. In the north we'll know what we're looking for. In the north we'll find a place where we can rest awhile. As you flip through the book on your lap I think back to another Before, a Before where we're just married and there is no you.

The week we were away stretches itself thin and wraps itself around our wrists. Days like speckled inlets and loops of sleeping and being awake. My eyes drift across the lawn through the particles of that glimmering week when I found out you were dying. Our elastic time contracted without concentrating. I remember hungrily recollecting to fill my lungs with every bit of air we'd ever breathed together. Recalling feelings and smells and over-exposed images that start to corrode near the edges. I remember how your hair smells just after you've washed it at the edge of those minutes before it dries. I also remember the nameless emotions I feel when you're with me. Those feelings aren't always good, but they're ours.

You're asleep in the passenger seat. An hour or so left before we get to the border. Out here there's almost nothing. Just stars and headlights and a few outlines of real clouds. No radio stations. We're so far from anywhere. I drive in silence and think back to another Before when we were traveling together into another night, not like this night at all. I held your hand and you were younger. I let go and I'm in a small white room looking out over low North American hills. Out on the rise a Cloud. I can still conjure fragments—I can still push my face against the glass of your memory. Here, at least for now, the Clouds can't see me. This North Dakota's border shifts again and confuses them, but they'll learn soon enough matching our steps to catch and eat us.

Farther into the northern dark a night that slips past the lowered hem of evening and on into the blue-black of the forest road in the hours after midnight. I think we might be lost but I don't care. Night's water is deeper now. It collars our necks as we wade out. I think about the stars as nickels fallen into a deep clear well with sunlight catching their dying sparkle as they flutter to an unseen floor. Some of these errant coins are in your eyes today. Soon your eyes will be all nickels and mine only water. I tell you we're lost. We keep driving in search of salvation. Through the inked-out sunroof we see the death masks of constellations.

They're moving me to another room today. The windows are much narrower and the sun falls in a stranger color on the floor. I try to keep track of our Befores in a notebook but sometimes they fall away through cracks in the wall and under doorways. Too many whispers and dusty oil paintings of South Dakota.

Now I think back to an even earlier Before, a time when I wasn't this person and when you weren't you and he was a long way from being born. I lived under those same constellations. In this memory I saw a different Before that called me by my human name and I smelled the sea caught in your hair. As I curled myself around myself in sleep I huddled closer into one more dream of you.

That night I dreamed of the you asleep in Wyoming's trees. The Bighorns halogened with autumned cottonwoods. These dreams are the last clues I have. I write them carefully in ruled notebooks. Knotted into the prairie night I played a few notes from your sequences on the just-out-of tune autoharp I took from an almost empty farmhouse near Gascoyne. Some faded coloring book pages and the tattered hem of a dress, a place of lives once lived before the world got away.

The first time I came to the human world I was born to Icelandic farmers in a valley near Holmavik. They were meant to have a different baby but I took it away before they knew. Now it's lost in another Before. The Icelanders knew about us a long time ago. They called us *huldufólk*. I grew older and fell into deadly love with a half-spectre, another kind of hidden person. Forever building tone-poems from wrecked fishing boats and curling her pale hair with sounds from puffin wings. I visited her in the hills near a waterfall. In the seventeenth year of my first life among humans I got sick and died in my bed. At the edge I called for her but her name could not be heard by humans and my voice was silent. Then, in a long hallway by myself holding a thick cardboard ticket with the number seventeen printed on it. Farther down the hall I could hear people swimming in a pool, its chlorine smells moving softly through the passageways. After what seemed like a few hours a crackly loudspeaker told me to take my ticket to the fourth door along the corridor. As I clicked the lock open I found myself wandering through snowy fields toward a gold-white papercut of light. Off in the wild distance, the stars played the notes of her name on a new winter mantle. And I waited patiently for seventeen years for the rest of you to find me.

Evening's particles fall. White gold. Snow accumulates around your feet as I whisper in your ear. I remember the words only as they're coming out of my mouth. I've traveled for days to get here—this island of you in the night. I walked in silence for years and the inside of my shoes got soaked with blood. The desert sky is clear and blue like a drawing of a lake made with colored pencils. I let a few more words fall from my mouth into the snow. They freeze at the edge of my lips and drop to the ground. The letters break apart, quickly whisked up in the cold Icelandic night. Move on. Into the dark, near farmhouses and sheep, I'm looking for you in any patch of moonlight I can find. I hear an arctic tern guarding her nest. I'm not sure if any of us had ever gone backward.

I drift through this Icelandic purgatory as a hungry revenant. Haunting another haunted landscape. Winding across the barren rock and my body now goes unseen in the fleshy world of pink cheeks and sea-breezes. I push deeper into the Westfjords where the echoes of burned witches and salt-stained fishermen are thick on the water. In a distant cottage at the edge of a crooked fjord she's waiting for me, writing a book made out of abalone shells and doubled-up mandolin strings. In another country of her soul a person unties a few packages, making her cry. Inside her, there is a city that moves and an office worker files another off-white folder.

You can never know about me. I live in long backward shadows. *Ur-shadows*, the shadows other shadows catch in side-long glances and in half-seen reflections on windowpanes. In these invisible and eternal afternoons, my hours are consumed in a little office, lower now than even the snaked-out subway lines. We make the Dreamers look like the ones they're hunting piece by piece. The rumble of the trains is comforting and sad. I think about her eyelashes moving dust motes through almost-slow-motion sunbeams. I think about it and it happens. And I make him fall in love with her and I make them live together in an old farmhouse in Vermont, a different Vermont. Another Wyoming of Vermont. They were fixing up the kitchen and then she died. And I'm unemployed. I'm packing up my office and taking down the photos of her ageless quietude, a gentle mirrored snowflake. She haunts and calls to me already. I'm on my way to find her, to send her back to haunt him if only as a dream. Hopefully he'll dream forever and never wake up. They can live in another Wyoming made out of their golden Vermont.

The parcels of emotions float helplessly in her veins. Northern-lake blood. She keeps writing with uncut abandon while the words and letters river out from under her fingernails onto the pages. White enamel and pointed roots wound up in eight steel wires. Out above the water the fulmars make tired circles in the air. This small patch of woods is where I thought I heard your voice. The night before I dreamed of a house that could have been ours—lemon trees and terrible blue skies. You told me to find you in the forest in another time and I came to rest in these silent and precarious woods. Equality cowboys the devil's tower.

Spider webs—the sunspace between leaves—warm pins of light. Waiting and hoping to see you pass through the edge of my vision. Or maybe a rustle in the dried leaves that tells me you're here. I saw you once in real-life and I felt like we'd been in love so many times before. Maybe you don't exist and maybe I'm lost and maybe I'm alone in the forest in this worn-out light of September. The sound you make isn't words but notes from a music box cut from wind. And then you're there. I still can't see you. Your verdant presence and your hair against the back of my ears. Your hiddenness injects itself into my memory and I mouth the letters of your name. I call you without words and you pass beside me in a whitish-yellowed glow like the pages in a very old book and lemon-colored Christmas lights colliding. You look over at me with a half-moon smile. A woozy slip in my bloodstream and I breathe a bit more deeply. I try to inhale you and then you're gone. Evaporated in the warmth that's unusual for this time of year.

Forever another Before. In this one I find you in the forest. One kiss. It's all so quick on the air and you're just one slippery moment in this earlier Before. On another High Plains wind, away in the night.

A held hand melts into air. I wanted to wonder about you. You lived in that house for two years and the notebooks kept piling up around you before they walled you in and you suffocated like Elizabeth Báthory bricked up in her own castle to die. Just to fade and drift away. Different sorts of blood sacrifice, I suppose. A pinprick to an ocean.

Another Before. I'm with my father on the other side of the border. The lake followed us step for step and mile for kilometer. Farther north there is another city made of close pulpy clouds and long summer evenings. Its grain elevators and alcoholic streets all but forgotten or ignored by the Clouds and the Dreamers. Sleeping giants to sleep forever in hard-worn tattoos. West into the land of the dead. Now the Western Lands. And Winnipeg slits its wrists into the Red River and goes on dying. Disappearances and other flickering memories press themselves against the car window. Rain falls as the asphalt becomes gravel as trees give way to wheat.

We dream about nights made of underwater museums. Ships' horns in the distance as we slip below the surface of our own waves. Strange insects move in the dark nearness as their sounds traveling in overlapping envelopes of summer noise, always balancing at the edge of my ear. I try to imagine what the evening glow of this house's inner organs must look like from the road. The door is warped and can't be closed from years of restless sleep. Into the hallway where books about Montessori, log homes, and wildflowers once sat on a narrow homemade shelf. I see your echo vibrate in the lengths of time as I stand there cataloguing the dissolution of another one of my worlds. The stars are so bright out here that I can almost feel their cold white heat on the back of my hands. The moon burns a long-lost fire. I turn and walk away to lie down in the tipped-back-as-far-as-it-will-go front seat of the car. This place is still contagious with memory not even close to the end of its half-life. My guts feel deep and spongy under my t-shirt and I imagine my blood's being replaced with a chemical sadness. A deadly lonesome transfusion. Moving west from the inland sea we were here and now I'm alone.

Before I was his son I was an owl. I wrote notes in moonlight and hid them in abandoned burrows. I rode on the North Wind's back and clipped the tops of old pines with my feathers. In the Western Lands dreams still hibernate.

Dark patches underwing. Here there are mapped locations and spaces but few peopled places. In the sky above a snowed-in field I see deeply below, into tomorrow. A man talks to me sometimes. He is lonely and lost in the world in himself. Stranded in looped memory. His sightlines cross oceans and states. Some of the colored flecks in his eyes are made of happiness, a bright-yellow feeling that sometimes passes me in flight. Memories and sadnesses rush past. Most of them I can forget or ignore but not his. His are heavy with a dream nailed into memory. He is a wild island underwing. He cannot be grounded among conifers and gravel roads. He imagines me. I am real. I become his voice on gray feathers and I search the blackness for light. For a path through the night and into the warmth of lighted bridges over quiet streams. Now in a dream he stands on the bridge where the gaslight flickers in near silence around him. Snow falls and turns into fireflies in the lamplight. In the distance a boy in moccasins and a blue ski sweater approaches on snowshoes. Another dream of fireflies. He wakes covered with soft light and his head resting on the papery South Pacific of a worn atlas covered with lines. Only some are imagined. Others in ball-point pen. It is cold in his house but he doesn't turn up the heat on his way to bed. He pulls the blanket around his shoulders. The radio plays Paul Simon with mystical certainty. The autumn night arches its almost-noiselessness and washes him back to dreaming. Wings on new snow. The daughter's fingertips are feathers. A golden wraith now shadows the windowsills.

I plastered my memories of you in the adobe and painted it yellow. Your tiny words keep this house together.

An evaporated cowboy and his Indian counterpoint share the wind that blows in from the North. I see them from our car window as we brush away California, roll through Wyoming, on into South Dakota. Wyoming has fewer people than Alaska and its lonely explosions thunder nightlessly. The Black Hills open up into a lodgepole evening. Deep unconsciousness and knotted space braid together. You think of this place and I think back to being young in other kinds of wheat fields. Before.

I looked out over Saskatchewan and on toward the edge of the Earth. Columbus never found the edge of the world, but he never made it to Saskatchewan. The wheat moves its hair over my face. I sit contentedly among the stalks. The sky is the darkest pre-storm blue. It'll be raining soon.

Depopulated and sad. Saskatchewan remembers only the dust of the super-grid roadways and the soundless cascade of falling farmhouses. The light is a different color here—overexposed and shot on expired film.

We're under Saskatchewan divided by lines and the absence of roads. We're going North. Flinging the night out into the rangeland. Just beyond the headlights the steppes of Wyoming curtain-call the spectral gas bars filled with clippings about rodeo prizes. The path we take winds the breeze around our necks and my father and I are alone in a world of high-beams and windshields. We're both prairie suns, burning out in a shattered midnight made from Van Morrison songs and bottled water from a Lakota Sioux reservation.

In time we will find ourselves as other selves. Still the same but different and lining our words with pine needles and lake water writing cursed tendrils through Minnesota forests. We keep driving deeper into the night. I look over my shoulder into the back seat where you've got a small pile of notebooks. I don't remember them being there earlier but maybe I wasn't paying attention. My father wants to see his boyhood home one last time and I want answers to questions about your illness. I get out my own notebook and I begin to read the things I wrote about you in another Before but I am tired and soon I'm dreaming my way back across Iceland. On a northern lakeshore highway we followed trails of aluminum night-lights. You'd fallen asleep with the notebook open on your lap and your head bumping lightly against the window. For a moment our Befores were almost parallel. Once or twice I saw you in the corner of my rearview mirror. I can't know how long she's been gone from my lives. The car pushes itself against the evening as we drive north. The iron ore mine pulsates with fluorescent dreams made out of too much not-sleeping and the loneliness of place. There aren't any deciduous trees here. Only tall isolation covered in blisters filled with spruce sap. You were sleeping. I noted each gravel road the headlights traced. I was looking for the right one, the road with a sign painted in dark red on pale yellow. I turned off of the pavement and the world disappeared in a fog of unmarked cars and the lacy roughness of balsam limbs. A tunnel on into the forest. The car is a Lada. License plate: JWA 1949. In the glove compartment was a hand-written note in Cyrillic script that read: "Our love is made from the soil of Ukraine, buried in the rings of poplars and in the teeth of the Hnila Lypa fish. Take this car to Enderlin in America and wait for me there. Love Hedeon." A warm bubble with lightbulbed arcs of numbers curses me deeper.

And still another Before. Dark blades clip the air cursing the breath that hides your words. The days unfurl in greater lengths as we go deeper into the forests of this old country. There are people in these woods who will know why you are dying. These Befores are always stillborn unremembered dreams. Again that Pull and I'm in another Before with you. Your chipped nail polish. I stare at your hands as they slip away in their apparent stillness, drawn up into the wintered womb of this poxed-out night. As you sleep in green foreign emptiness I draw an invisible heart-shaped map on your shoulder with my fingertip, careful not to wake you. Then I'm back in the car hurtling through northern Minnesota as I see the prickly possibility of morning crawl over the evergreens. Soon the pines are replaced by cyrilla and moriche palm. The air is thick with new kinds of insect sounds and our car is a dugout canoe with a cracked-paint outboard motor.

In a Southern jungle a huddled group of dwellings emerges from the wet dark of leaves. The sound of hushed pale voices. In the morning we'll travel upriver where the jungle forms a cottony haircut of mist. Tonight you'll sleep in a quiet made out of syrupy medicines. I wonder how I ever argued with you about pointless things. Tonight you're still living on the edge of warm blood. On the island of the dead you are *from away*—you don't belong with them. Or to them. You stand at the shore and wait for headlights in the forest. A canopy of tropical moths allows arrows of light that trace words from an unknown language across your skin. Having lifted myself out of that hope all I have now are crowded dreams and midnight rustlings in the underbrush.

Love like a Soviet apartment block: long wide full of tiny windows and dusted with concrete sadness. A thread of blood on the hand that balances on the gunwale. Out into the leaves and their houses and I see the forest's green mirrored on your cheek. Tiny planets of your blood falling carefully into the brown water as bits of your DNA collect along the river's bed. Your name in letters cannot be written in these strands. A flowering smile and your complicated smell are deeply etched on your cell walls. Everything's always almost somewhere but it never quite gets there: browning, calming, falling. The world moves and we are still. We're close now. A sphere of birds encompasses the boat. And in the here-before-we-know-it distance I see the leaves move aside as the Cloud swallows us whole.

The other side is cold and we look different. You're resting your head on my shoulder as the bus splits the burned-out sunlight reflected in glaciers. I step back in time and out of this heart-shaped moment. I see our hands and our place between them. The calm salty sweet of the ocean rubs up against my leg like a cat. Between our hands clasped tightly in youthful unawareness there are echoes of other Befores ripping back and forth. Tearing at each other's hair. I watch the black landscape made by tired volcanoes as it ticker-tapes alongside the forever-flat ring-road. We've been given one more reprieve, one more chance to unroll our dreams. While you sleep I look through the notebook that was left for me on the seat but it's written in a language I don't understand. Glued onto the last few pages I find several faded newspaper clippings about the disappearance of Amelia Earhart. In Iceland there are shells that wash ashore. In another Before I put one against my ear and listened for the Minotaur's call to arms—not yet too early. And again I'm back driving through the night beside a great lake, watching the edges of the headlights for moose and deer.

The owl turns on the wind to fly south to Guyana. In radiant Befores he saw the river.

Along the quieting lakeshore. Out in the fluid blue-black night. The half-empty moon like street lights exploding just below the water's surface. The old sturgeon buffers his eyes in the emergent glow and the songs of long-dead silver miners echo across the Now. Your nose has a slightly odd shape—a gently upturned leaf and I hear the sound of your country's plants when you speak. Not in the words but in the spaces between syllables. Openings like roughcut keyholes. Your face and voice change more often now. Before you were more constant but now closer to the end I see all of the other Befores and all of our memory palaces projected on your chalky skin. I stare so intently at you these days, a golden violence. Before I can tell you I'll miss you we're walking holding hands in the October wind of North Dakota. Between our hands a galaxy of restlessness. The bus slips into the Western night and as a hidden morning light sweeps thoughtfully over the other passengers picking them up and putting them into dreams netted by Senegalese fishermen seventeen years in the future. I wonder if she can see me like this and I feel uncomfortable. "Who is she?"—in the margin of my ruled notebook.

I'm sitting in a hospital in Dakar breathing in the forever multiplying sicknesses of New Africa. We were following the book and its lines to an old version of Senegal. How could we know? The man shot my father dead in the street. One of the dreaming diseases made him do it. A draft-dodger from The Mount Rushmore State, he lay dying in the powdery roadway, dirt from other places and times in the creases of his face and jeans. A fake tooth burning with red-brown blood and then he's gone. Just so, he's borne up onto the perfect hollowness of a Badlands wind that moves across the ocean. He didn't have to see how rough things got.

The inside of the hospital wasn't white as I'd imagined it. Beiges and grays with weird splinters of unknown color. My father is dead. I saw his sun-dried denim soul leave his body in a cloud of diesel vapor. A spectral notebook that's been following me through some of the most recent loops finds its way into my jacket pocket and turns into a dusty highway of yellow road signs paint chips. An asphalt neverland. Walking away from the hospital in Senegal, the dirt writes stories about forgotten states: Nebraska, South Dakota, Wyoming, Iowa, Minnesota, mostly North Dakota. Places that got eaten-up in the Shift. Dreamers didn't want them and let the Clouds chew them up. In another prairie-colored Before a train comes to rest at a crossing just outside Fargo. I turn the car around and head deeper into the grassland's opening-up black and away from the collected works of the Dreamers. Grain elevators gone cold. Ex-towns where one streetlight burns away at the dark. Only one light to push back the leopard's whisper. The old cat speaks under his breath as I pass the post office. In my dead father's language he tells me to guard myself against the hungry lions of this newly long winter night. His claws are worn and his once-sharp teeth are only mistreated shadows. Too many years of eating this wheat. Too many years of tearing at the funeral veil of night. In the leopard's father-voice I hear him say we've been careless and now it's too late. And then North Dakota gets forgotten. Only a part of the United States on cardboard globes from the 1950s and outdated maps from highway rest stops and empty classrooms. North Dakota floated out of their geography a few years ago and now it hovers flat and forgotten in the sky. At the edge of town, out past the abandoned Ukrainian Orthodox church I look over the state line down into the night and onto a bruised map, a purple-black hole on the uncurve of the High Plains. I wonder how the train ever made it this far and I turn my felt-lined boots back toward the hotel. Its kerosene warmth throws golden frequencies that lost sons and old leopards find hard to resist.

A morning. I wake up somewhere in the middle of the notebook. A blackened maze of forest beside a narrow moss-edged path. In the early sun between the pages I see animal shapes rummaging through words and sentences nibbling at semicolons and hyphens. I hear the toothless leopard in my blood and I remember my father and Senegal and the night seventeen years in the future when North Dakota rises out of the prairie in a snow-colored hymn. Or a freshly caught Dream, clouded over. A message from another Before, bottled and anchored with river blood.

Paper animals catch the morning light moving along trails worn through the notebook's forest of my thoughts. I sit there in our collective silence as if inside a large bell: quiet beyond belief and pregnant with resonance. I sit and watch the sounds that leave the animals' mouths in black felt-tipped lines. A sound-mark swirls up through the trees and takes the shape of a sleeping possum, wiry drawings accumulating in his velvet belly.

Inside Possum's stomach the drawings tell the story of a man living in an Old Era Iceland. The drawings are of standing stones on birchless islands and a longing for home. The story is unread and Possum pushes his little hands together to cup the Black Hills, en route to Saskatchewan.

The thick wind moves outside again. It's quiet on this side of the window. Outside there's a wilderness of feral sound. Rain doesn't fall in Iceland. It moves where the wind takes it—broken up into tiny fragments that press themselves against the corrugated metal of Ísafjörður's pockmarked houses. This diagonal weather is tonight's. It's 10:16 and the sun is still up. The always-already gray of this ripped-up island crouches down and peers into windows all across the Westfjords like some weird night-creature from the Sagas. My story is a bit like a ruled and dog-eared saga. Less bloodshed, fewer kings.

Even the colorful paint of the pre-school walls outside my window can't drive the gray away. The sky is a steel shadow outlined by the edges of disappointed buildings. I see the tops of people's heads float by on the street. I'm a bit higher up in my apartment so I can't see their faces but I'm pretty sure they're not smiling because they know there won't be any sunlight tonight. Another late December.

I try to imagine what it must be like to live here all the time. Lonely but also kind of beautiful in its longing winter dream. Iceland was like a China-doll-faced prostitute writing the world's most perfect novel in a spiral-bound notebook. Her outside is warm with thick breaths and fingerhook beckoning that brim with bloodless memories. Her insides are cold deserts full of rocks to cut your hands if you fall.

I'm holding your hands trying to pick the pinhead gravel out of the scrapes on your palms. Your blood like sap. I can see you trying not to cry. A small tear escapes and explodes on the back of my hand. Paper towel run under the tap to wipe away the blood. I think you're crying not from the pain but because you know what comes next. You're afraid because you're dying and my simple affection can't keep you afloat anymore. I hold your hands because they're bleeding but also because I don't want you to leave me here. Again. Before.

That summer I traveled to another Iceland in search of the lei lines that cross the bullwhipped face of its rocky interior. This part of the world burns with a holy hope that bristles and rings out across the cold salted water. I search the sides of cliffs and the low valleys for signs of the Hidden People and their underworld. If I can find this place then I can bring you there and hide you from this ever-changing disease. There must be some truth in fairytales. A little flower, a blue one.

A dream last night: more Clouds that hung in low heavy fog over the Westfjords. Through their vapors until I felt lightheaded, about to faint. I inhaled memories of you into my blood to carry you in my veins. Back to my heart. Back to before the Shift. And you're far away on the other side of some reckless body of water. And you're losing bits of life daily. Life trickles out when you're sitting on the toilet, when you open your mouth, when you're sleeping. Quietly while you're sleeping maybe you're the author of the Clouds filtered into my sleep and into our world. A gauzy telephone call made from water droplets hung carefully with night's clothespins.

Haunted between these shallow mountains. Not by something malicious. By the pale wild of abandoned farmsteads whispered into my skin. They told me about you and my body tore itself open in silence with something a thousand times purer and more elemental than love. You're dying everywhere at once and nowhere forever. Your warm yellow light followed me out here.

I'm watching you brush your hair in the smudged mirror of the upstairs bathroom. Three lights across the top of the medicine cabinet. One of the bulbs is missing. A band of darker light shadows your body. Your borders are on fire and the light in the bathroom slips easily off your skin into the night. You breathe out clouds filled with so many old kinds of electricity. Vapor-shapes pause on my forearms for a moment before their particles tunnel back into my blood. Indivisible tattoos. Tonight I'm watching you brush your hair for one more last time.

You died on a Saturday. No more wind. No more falling leaves. No more insects. No more heartbeats. No more birds or dogs. No more music boxes.

Before the Shift you were young and pulpy, tipped like a poison arrow with pure emerald being. We lived in loops of our own design, not these broken circles of Now. We traveled between cities and states through dreams held close in afternoon naps. We poured our wishes into photographs and ink. This Us existed in a past now aged to yellow. Only the asphalt now knifes its way through my memory. I'm driving alone, north on what's left of Highway 61 looking for one of the openings I read about in the notebook. I can't see anything through the snowstorm. I pull into a gas station parking lot. I fall asleep in a nest of crumpled dreams.

In one of these Minnesota dreams I followed the curved gravel road of your silhouette. Waves, the sound of seagulls and the smell of rotting leaves and cedar tried to comfort the disquieting air. Dusty auroras wrestled in the last spindles of our sunset. I squeezed your hand a bit too tightly because I knew I'd never see you again once the evening erased itself again. Another never Before. As we walked you told me about the places you'd dreamed before.

We talked about these places. Ships borne up on white lightning rivers. We turned topography and correspondence inside out but there were no more clues and no more allegations. The papers you'd found in the attic were birthed before they'd come to term. A stillborn life held in our hands scratched out in fading cursive loops. Loops of untamed time of loops of loops and on and on. Now most of the words and sentences have evaporated into Clouds that curdle above summer and its yellow and white gingham buttonups. And then you were gone. Vaporized in the contagious sunlight from another Before. Alone again with my headlights staring out into the night. The next town on my list is Valentine, Nebraska.

We'd been on the road for almost two months following the writings my father had kept hidden from me all these years. Across the Dakotas and Wyoming to Saskatchewan and down to New Mexico. We trailed after the half-formed sentences and hurriedly sketched maps from the notebooks. Every day fewer words and letters remained. We chased after vanishing ideas written in a dying language forgetting and remembering the fractured grammar we traveled.

The wind spilled through the streets. An invisible and cinematic tidal wave carrying its cargo of broken marriages and red-brown dust. It pushed through the tree lined avenues and empty shopping arcades of a nowhere-is-everywhere city. One of the first Clouds appears on the rotten gold horizon.

A hotel in another prairie town. Always searching for answers evaporating into the dry summer air. A square faced building with rooms on the second floor—weird rooms with indescribable histories of blown out water stains and half wild smells. I was sitting at the edge of the open window looking down into the flow of ghost pickups and garbage particles. The Wind's voice tangled in my hair and started telling stories picked from blue water and sand dunes, dying freedom fighters and woeful crocodiles. Stories about death and islands and downed planes in an unknown atoll's thinning jungle, the kinds of dreams from the bottom of the world lying next to the letters of your name or some other ancient word from an old Before. Another wobbly wornout tape loop.

In another Before that is definitely not mine the Wind is a woman in a painting of South Dakota. She's lost in time in the types of grasses that don't remember names. She looks out to the place where pale blue borders yellow-brown. There are invisible foxes in her painting. They hide in the places where Christmas lights won't reach. The accumulated presence of the woman lines up like sunbeams in our apartment in a different Dakota.

This is how the story begins and ends. You can't be here with me. The house is a palimpsest and the drapes are only the edges of dresses in museums now. There are calls coming in from overseas. They can wait. The telephone rings like it does in films about old-fashioned police detectives. The only voices out here on the sea are mine and the Wind's. My voice reminds me I'm already dying and maybe I've died before. The Wind tells me it'll be okay and I should let this sleep take me a bit farther out into the part of the ocean where the waves are bigger and where even extra long telephone cords won't reach.

As the other Before gets swallowed by seawater behind me I keep walking thinking that I'll eventually suffocate in the drift of wheat and winds coming in from the West. I don't stop breathing and I don't get lost. After two days of moving through this strange topography I arrive in a town that's been hidden for hundreds of years. I can't go home. I restart a life-loop in this new and nameless numberless place. I'm trapped in happiness but it's someone else's happiness—always someone else. By now I've stopped counting the hours (days?) since we lost each other on the North Dakota prairie. In an earlier Before, the doctor looks at me through spotty glasses while you hold my hand and trace the edges of my cuticles with your fingernail. He's talking about cell counts and bone marrow. The words are dull and lukewarm as they leave his mouth. You're writing an outline of another Before in your notebook, one that skims the surfaces of South Dakota and layers its scars in the state's unnamed dirt.

As this Before is written into a notebook in a hospital it flutters to life in the Badlands. Her desert rose skirt hangs quietly over the edge of the bar stool in this no-such-place. A forever fleeting Western town. There's a road through here that leads Away but I doubt you'll ever find it. This town is hot with dried dirt and a thousand paint flecks from out-of-print RVs and out-of-place Italian motorcycles. A state without a name. A town without a sound. I wonder how they—the Americans—live next to us without knowledge of our movements and the sounds we make at night. Our secret plan takes shape quietly in your night. This town is West of everywhere and that woman's skirt—its brittle hem—is the blade that cuts between known and unknown. In our state dreams form inside a perfect rectangle.

I write the State Story. I write the dreams in letters and draw loops of tangled sunlight around odd rock formations in the desert. I sit here in my house at the edge of town—at the edge of the state. I write this story for nobody. I write about our travels our houses our kisses our deaths. Words in a language with no spoken sound like abandoned campfires and refrigerators with the doors off their hinges, hanging like time. In this place there is no sense in loneliness. The haunted geography surrounds me and turns into a kernel of wheat at the bottom of a grain elevator. I turn another page in my notebook and follow the pen back across the page.

The story writes itself along dark desire lines. It flies in wild directions earnestly brushing a piece of hair from her forehead. In the next instant swiftly unfurling itself into frozen isolation. Some days I imagine this island might be somewhere near Antarctica. It isn't that cold here and there aren't any National Geographic photographers or penguins. Something about the vastness of the sea and the feeling of the air makes me think that we're close to the bottom of the world. I don't know how long I've been here. Reading the stories of my life from notebooks I don't remember writing. There are no calendars or clocks that I can understand. There are no atlases or maps of this place. All I know is that it's called Miro and that there hasn't been a bird here in over four hundred years. And nobody seems to know about the Shift or the Old Era.

In a different Before I pick the golden minutes from the spruce tree near our house. The lower branches now dead and covered with bluish-gray globules of sap. These plastic limits of our remaining time hang in suspense like stranded jellyfish or tiny clouds of wintered breath in a different Vermont. I loop back down the far side of the hill through the snow and trees and back up the road that runs along the edge of our property. The lane that leads up to our place half-circles itself down another little rise. At the bottom of this bump of earth just before the house I can see all the way to Miro Island. Only for a shiver of a minute. There aren't any lights on in the house tonight. As I walk back to the lightless building I remember one of your more recent deaths.

I loop my arms around your shoulders in the back of the old car. Your breathing thickens. I tell you it's only a few more miles to the hospital. I kiss your forehead. The Northeast Kingdom's moon hurls itself across the lake and in through the window. You're fading out brightly tonight. In another Before, and in a Before that's never Vermont, there are loops that move in bent waves across all of our different lives. At the edges of those lives we were closer to each other than we ever knew. Now we're anchored in a forest of things and moments that have never and already happened.

At the house a few days later I pick up one of the notebooks to read through more of your dreams. Dark light purls in the margins. An ocean washes unknown species of driftwood onto the beach at the limit of our world. The light here is new and old together. The color of early morning dreams: pink-gray with round quiet shadows. Our boat with its six oars skims the precipice where the sea falls into nothing. The sound of the wooden blades on the water makes a muffled and angled rhythm. We are four. We are *the* four. A Christopher Columbus waves us ashore with his tattered cuffs poking out from the sleeves of his dust jacket. Yellowed words dulled by time. On the beach at the last stop of the world. Across water the color of broken windows I can see you again. A crumbling detective novel and a small pile of faded inky letters at your feet. A sign for the museum hangs from a lone evergreen. This island is infinite in its smallness, as if it could shrink forever, always finding new ways to compress itself into little packets of languages no longer spoken.

The detective novel you were reading was set in Iceland. It was about a pair of sisters who worked at a gas station in the Westfjords and their plot to kill a local sheep farmer who was responsible for their father's death at sea. The killer had never been charged because their father's death had been ruled an accident. The sisters knew otherwise. I picked up a few of the novel's errant letters and pushed them against my cheek. The sentences they'd once formed slipped quietly into the corner of my mouth and I spoke the second story of the book as it was first written in the secret language of the hidden people. And still as always the shores of the Great Lake clawed themselves deeper north. The sisters felt lonely in this unknown province. In another Before up along Lake Winnipeg to Hecla Island. They'd heard that their father's killer lived on Black Island and they'd marked him for trial in their new miniature Wyoming. The Wind turned cold and the blonder sister pulled her homemade scarf tight around her snowed-in neck.

With the last of them gone I was alone. Moss and tundra. My heart was deep-set with a detuned longing. I was the last of Iceland's hidden people. A disease has haunted us for almost a hundred years now as it ushers us quietly into non-existence and erases our presence. I think we caught it from sharing your language. Once we started speaking your words we got weak and soon we were trying hopelessly to cut the hidden tumors from our hidden bodies. The things that killed us hid in the same way that we hide from you. We weren't always hidden. We used to live in your blood and under your eyelids but you pushed us out and sent us into the mountains and fjords. Now we die invisibly from your disease. My imagined feet soundlessly crush moss and blue flowers on this hillside near Holmavik.

Last night I dreamed New Iceland in Canada on Lake Winnipeg. Away. I sealed the dream in a zip-top bag with a small stone and I threw it into the North Sea.

This Before is a time before Befores when the Earth was made out of different sounds. Other kinds of light. I'm back from Reykjavik driving with my father past hollow rest stops through the abandoned nights of rural Minnesota. Sleepily he thinks back to a different time and catalogs it carefully among his other F-stopped dreams.

On my brother's couch the light goes out. Tonight I am old. I am revolutionary. I am revenge. I am the freed spirit. I am a forest-walker. I am the Alone Ranger at the Gates. I hurt in my wrist and in my heart. I am thinning. I am the path to the river that passes under the farmer's orange electric fence held up so you could crawl through. I am a young navy blue t-shirt as the sun starts to set over the other field. I am your father and I am wild and sad. I dream my children into golden vignettes beside a lilac tree in the front yard. She wants to go but I tell her to wait while I take a few more photos. An unnamed presence pulls the dark around me a little tighter as I sleep into next year. Snow starts to fall. Merry Christmas: a white bear. Under the purposeful neon of the Northern Lights a cloud-colored bear drifts on the pack ice off the coast of Newfoundland. Some time in the night he passes Baffin Island and his ice-raft lifts itself up and out of this Before into another. In the following morning's light he is waking up on a pebbly beach at the edge of a writhing river that overflows with salmon. His whiteness rips holes in the green and brown of the Alaskan wilderness and he starts to see pictures of the man in his head.

Farther up the hills past the Clouds that curl over the city, there's a floating point of land. On this wayward piece of Earth: a mountain, a lake, a valley, a man. He lives alone on the island surviving on blueberries and cattail roots. His island is an exile from the memories of her. He draws maps and charts in his notebooks always trying to find his way back to that other Before. He didn't always live here, he was brought here to die a few years ago. Set adrift above St. Paul and Duluth in a valley that's hidden by real clouds. He sat at the edge of the island and tried to remake the patchwork memories of a girl he'd loved in another Before.

We've been surrounded by birch trees all our lives—their leaves make music from north winds. On the shore of this mountain lake snow falls earlier than in the valley. A hundred pebbles under your moccasined feet and I can hear the roll of your heel in the way you walk. The only noise I dream of out here on this island. Only sand—tiny particles won't give up their noises to anyone for anything.

Up here I'm closer than anyone else to the northern lights. At times their colors burn out the sky. Glowing in thick waves across the inked-out night. As they pulse me to sleep I hope I'll meet you again at the edge of your other dream.

I'm always a part of the dream but I'm still not sure if it's mine. It's not hard to get caught in other people's dreams. In these unfamiliar dreamworlds our costumes are frayed and ill-fitting but we still act out our parts hitting our marks well into morning. In this dream I'm myself but unlike my waking world self. I'm one degree off. One more click on the dial. The path that leads to the edge of the lake is the same. The trees and shrubs that line it are unfamiliar. I hear your voice (who are you?). A badger crosses the trail and my eyes follow his low-slung body as it rustles off into the woods. Unsuccessfully I try to wake up. This is your dream. This is what happens when two people sleep with their heads too close. I'm in disguise. Maybe you don't recognize me. Along the beach and over seaweed-covered rocks I make my way to where you're standing. The water isn't very deep and soon I'm beside you looking out over the water into the faded midnight sun. We don't look at each other. We just stare out over the water—out over the water to my head and my pillow and my dream. I look down at your feet under the rippling lake water. So white. Grains of sand rush across your toes. The bottom of your dress is damp and bits of dead leaves assemble on the hem.

I'm staring at the dark patches the little lake waves have soaked into the bottom of your dress. A freshwater darkness follows the outline of southern Russian borders—a line of broken leaf parts marks the Urals— that forever division between West and East. Moving closer I'm drawn into the wet gray cotton and before I can pull away I'm caught in the waves of your skirt and then I'm on some unnameable Eastern Bloc street walking past a sad old dancing bear toward a bunch of worn-out dreams on the edge of Moscow.

In the far corner of the flea market, past all the fakes and cast-offs, a few small tables push up against a crumbling brick wall. This is where the Russian girl and her father keep their posters. She and the old man sell scraps of the revolution. Shreds of broken-down socialist glory. The Russian girl holds the sun behind her ear as it spills down through a torn plastic canopy on its way to her summer-blue eyes. Her wheat-colored hair is a Ukrainian field in August: tied into a braid, a loose twist that moves more than she does. And now I see her across the field beside the fence that marks the division between the reactor and the waving snowdrifts of grain. She's dressed in a folk costume made out of velvet and gilded with ribbons. Slices of brocade fall into place between her movements. Miniature gestures. A prayer flag in Buryatia.

Moscow's last wasps of summer hover at the edge of my drink. I wonder how and when I fell this far into the looping folds of her dress and why I'm sitting beside a Russian street market in a Before that's unimaginably distant from my other Wyoming. I can't remember how long I've been traveling inside her dreams or where she's taken me after all these months (years?). Every so often I get a little glimpse of Miro through an open window in some wood-and-mud town in the afternoon sun at the end of a one-way street but then it's gone and her face changes again.

Among the many-authored winds of this people's republic, I stand and stare at the flag blooming in a silent night across darker wilder landscapes. She can't see her other Before but I can and I know I've been beside her in at least two other Befores. I remember her wearing the folk costume riding the train to Odessa for a state-sponsored cultural performance. I rested my face against her shoulder and the smoothness of the silk filled my blood with a pearled wilderness. In Buryatia now we search the night sky for provinces above the clouds. All we see are cooling stars and blue-black moonlight. North Dakota hovers at the edge of Lake Baikal just out of sight. The leopard and the son look over the edge of this floating bit of the High Plains and watch the train. Her face is a vapored crescent in one of its low-lit windows.

Snow blue of night in this floating Wyoming of North Dakota. The evening falls in folds like old curtains from a drawing room in some make-believe English country estate. I can see in the edge of the moon's light that you cringe a little each time we hear a bit of gravel hit the underside of the car. Outside the world is freezing solid, crystalizing in our wake—a jeweled sarcophagus for our memories. Beyond the car's interior it's violently winter again and the clarity of a just-before-Christmas cold is everywhere. There isn't any snow on the ground—this year's been weird that way. We round the bend and I tell you I think it's near here and I just need to find the little orange sign my father painted years ago. Time bunched-up like wildflowers and handed over roughly without a vase. I've come back to this northern place to see the wilted memories I still pay property taxes on. Nobody lives here and our memories are running low on supplies. They're almost just birch trees now.

I uncover the banjo my parents got as a wedding present. It's hidden behind some crumply blueprints with penciled-in numbers and arrows. A few more things to salvage. Out in the garden I see an image of myself holding a bunch of beets. It must be sometime in August. Probably around my birthday. And then we drive back to the city in the northern light that turns summer into evening—along a paved road that leads me away from the time when my hair was still blond. We pass tiny corner stores that sell overpriced once-a-year cans of pumpkin pie filling and fishing licenses.

Sporadic halogen lights on the evening blacktop of the highway that runs through our country. More streetlights for nobody. They don't run along this roadway's entire length. Pinpricked at certain spots where you might turn off the road into a town made out of particle board and the smell of boiled wood pulp. A girl works at the video store beside the lake. Her hands are rougher than the Russian daughter's and her nails are ragged and bitten down. Her hair is a color that is not the color of the Russian daughter's. Her dreams make a noise most of us can't hear. Just plain cotton quiet. The Russian daughter's fingertips are crow's wings beating against the snow. Do you see it over the White Ridge down past the Frozen Creek up the Wintered Lane? There's a house cut out of the night by firelight and inside-warmth. Up in the house there are parties and fights. Really it's just one party and just one fight and the fight is about smashed-up love and the party is a warped Chet Atkins record spinning lopsided forever deeper into the evening. Sometimes the Russian daughter hears the Chet Atkins record but because she has no frame of reference it quickly turns into the sound of a Lada engine in Yakutsk.

In an earlier Moscow the Russian daughter keeps a secret book of pictures of old houses in Vermont with tall wooden lines that speak to her in uncommon dialects, a once-dreamed vernacular in paper valleys. Sometimes she rests her ear against the cool glossy pages. And she hears the music coming down over the snow-covered hill. She's dreaming of another house—one that isn't in her book—out in Wyoming near Lusk. Maybe it's the last one. Beauty lives there too. Other clumsier shapes—terrible and fragile. To cut and ache. But she's still sleeping.

Some of the dreams are made out of things we found around the house: the Great Plains sunlight in your haphazard ponytail and old posters from a flea market in Moscow form almost-seen shadows and reflections. Your nap got cut short by the crackle of gravel in the driveway as our dream instantly began to unwind. Our Dreamers were here. Even this far out they found us. Pieces of our lives swirled around us, splashing loudly into the pond behind the woodshed and flinging themselves against walls. From the upstairs window I saw them step out of an old truck as the world collapsed. Their polished shoes caught the lures of afternoon's light once more. I stumbled down the splintering stairs. Rushing to wake you up. No more gentle lines of dust particles, no more prairie sleep. You were gone for seventeen years—I counted them out in dreamless summers. And again you're gone into another Before and now I trace your paths through time and forever farther out into the ocean. How did I escape? I didn't.

In the seventeen winters of those summers I followed lines of blood through the snow to hospitals for people with hearts-too-wild. Maybe this is where they took you. Most of these places aren't listed in phone books. Some of them aren't signed at the top of driveways that don't lead down quiet winding paths to bucolic country mansions. I looked for you in these places for seventeen years. I called clueless strings of numbers my children and constantly pulled that Icelandic scarf tighter around my face to ward off the hungry North Dakota wind. They say you can tell good wool if it still smells a bit like sheep. This wool must be good. Why didn't the places where I looked for you smell like hospitals?

The smell of hospital—fresh-peeled self-adhesive bandages. Now this part of the hospital is deserted at night. I stare at the outline of the doorframe illuminated by the hallway lights. I've been here for a length of time. I can't understand what I'm suffering from. Tonight I'll dream about West Virginia. Will you come looking for me? And if you see me, call me by my older name.

That night I sleep in the waiting area on a chair made out of a creaky blue plastic. My father's leopard voice echoes in my head ringing out along an almost-imaginary fjord.

Over the lake and away from the ocean, caught between the feathers of an old white owl, the light rides out into the dark. Past the snowed-under hills and through the tree-shadows there is a man alone in the forest. He's part of the nothingness that's full to overflowing. On and on into the burning moonlit air with tiny lives fractured below and caught in the drafts that scurry under farmhouse doors. Now the owl is out of sight and the man keeps walking down the turned-up lane to his house. The noise of snow under his feet is filled with loneliness. The spruce trees do their best to comfort him with their outstretched arms. He feels alone but he's surrounded by an invisible and exploding love. He stumbles through another winter evening. Christmas lights haunt the points on the roof. Holiday will-o-the-wisps with tails made out of green plastic wire. Some of the paint on the older bulbs has chipped away. More gap-toothed stars. The quiet crushes into his chest and weighs on his aging eyes.

And then the story of my sedimentary life. There are parts taken from other Befores and from Befores that haven't happened yet. It's a story written inside a circle told by an Icelandic crow. I've translated his calls with careful dead mathematics.

The island road is rough and filled with large stones. The bus tires pick their way slowly through the bumps and holes while old women eat black beans from repurposed plastic margarine containers. Little children with skin the color of cowboy boots stare out the windows onto landscapes they've seen a hundred times. And here we are, following more translations and ill-conceived maps from the always-dissolving writings of another Before. You have the book tucked under your arm and I can see the place where your tan meets your other skin at the edge of your t-shirt. A fragment of text delivered us to the side of a volcano in another wet-hot forest. From Icelandic to English, our piece of writing describes a path through the trees to a waterfall. The way to find the next collection of stories about her life and death. About the writing that you've left for me. I'll write them in my notebook and add them to the others that have accumulated over the past few years. Maybe soon I'll know enough of the words to start putting it together, and then maybe I can find the openings to some of the other Befores, always out of reach where you're already always waiting.

Right now I'm the memory of a crow that died in 1968 and my life and its end are far more important than anyone can ever know.

The crow was, before, another cat.

In the Before when I was another cat I lived in Gimli, Manitoba and I belonged to a woman named Edda. I remember eating bits of whitefish on the back step in the summer. Edda's husband Einar died from a liver disease before I came to stay with her. She'd often tell me how much she missed his wool coat that used to hang in the front hall. In that Before I buried a shard of Wyoming in the pebbles on the beach—just a particle. Only a fragment of the emptied plains. A golden placeholder.

Deep in the Christmas of a sad little mall in upstate New York. All around me the whirling mess of plastic bags and light that isn't real. I feel like maybe I remember real light—the sun's light. I'm wrapped around myself, alone, save for the unwatched child that pokes me through the wire cage. I'm another homeless cat lifted from the streets and institutionalized. I'm abandoned and on display. They hope someone will adopt me. I'm not much of a kitten anymore and I'm thick. Tired of this world once more. I write this memory to myself in my sleep. I write these memoirs of being a homeless cat in the mall at Christmas from my cage while I seem to sleep. I have nothing but time and I sleep a lot these days.

I dropped the piece of paper and then to my knees in the snow. Out of the woods into the moon-filled clearing and you're holding my hair against your jacket's pearled buttons. You asked me why I was crying. I told you I had been a cat in another Before. Now I knew how our world would fade into nothing but poisoned memories. Those half-remembered dreams of all the never-Befores hacked to bits in the night.

We held hands under more northern auroras. A pine martin watched with tiny black eyes. I remember the smell of your left cheek in the winter. The cold changes odors and draws new circles around them in my mind.

Not long after that night in the field you were another echo. I never saw you sitting at the end of our bed—nothing like a glowing see-through outline with sad eyes. I never felt a cold spot in the kitchen where you used to sit by the window and watch the crows eating from the compost. You were the most beautiful parasite of my memory. You haunted my dreaming and my waking from somewhere behind my eyes.

This photograph smells like you. The back of it is coated with a constellation of notes and chords that describe the way your hair smells at five in the afternoon. Two-day old cotton next to your skin in late summer. The Northwest's rain haunts the photo's chemical colors. The crease in the corner resonates a life in the back of a drawer made out of laminated wood. I think about the shadows of our affection that never met sunlight or autumn and I wonder if there was something I could have done to save you. Maybe before. Not now.

In the months after your death, I studied maps of the South Pacific trying to memorize the names and locations of all the little island countries. All of the atolls and archipelagos. Pitcairn, Norfolk, Henderson. I tried to bend the gravity of my feelings for you into another loop of rope I could throw into the sea to rescue you. It didn't work. I booked a spot on a cargo ship traveling from Panama to New Zealand hoping to forget the Before I'd become once again. Of course you were welcome to come with me and I knew you would.

Luckily I was given my own cabin aboard the *Nebraska* and it proved fairly easy to continue our translation of the text without being disturbed. I hoped to have had the majority of the work done by the time we reached Pitcairn on December 7th but this wouldn't be the case as I soon became occupied with the translation of another more compelling document I'd discovered in one of the bulkheads.

I wondered what it would be like to vanish. I'd once heard the story of a friend's friend's brother who went to London for a vacation and never returned only to call several years later from Prague. I'd often wondered what had happened to make him want to disappear like that. What myths had accumulated in his absence? Soon I'll know. I'm gone tonight—you'll never see me again. I might write you periodically but you can never know where I am. This is my story of being forever and never. Being the first and last.

Postcard: a picture of a Galapagos tortoise
Postmark: Pitcairn Island, South Pacific
It reads: "Chernobyl loop #17. Amelia Earhart"

I didn't die in the crash—a broken wrist and a long cut on the back of my left arm. There are people here but they are unlike any I've ever known in both their customs and appearance. I can only see water. The island is about one mile wide by two miles long and the weather has been calm and warm every day since I arrived. I've become accustomed to life in this place and have even been given a small house at the end of one of the many narrow gravel roads that cover the island. I haven't seen anyone come or go and I'm unaware of the current date. There are no functional clocks or calendars on Miro.

Locations. Points on a map. Dots of varying sizes. For the past nine years you've only been shifting lines and circles of cartography. Cities inhabited by your glass teeth and pale eyes. When I knew you were really gone my insides started to crumble away. The train stations in places like Raton, New Mexico bleed a dry blood that mixes easily with dirt. I touch it with two fingers and rub it against my thumb. I say it's still warm (to myself) knowing it's always warm. This morning I think I found a strand of your hair at the edge of a gas station bathroom mirror somewhere in a forgotten Iowa. I found a tooth that was probably yours in one of our southern Oregons.

I'm trailing your jet-stream of illnesses across an American plain. The snowflakes in Minnesota become dying stars as I drive up 61 toward the border. In another Before that comes after this one we might do this same drive without the snow. At the edge of evening it's unseasonably warm and we've been friends since before I was born. That Before has yet to come. I'm alone in this one and searching for something different and lonely in the snow's bridal veil. Snowflakes trace the car and I drive further into the slippery quickness of the road and my memory. I'm remembering our first Christmas together in that Vermont.

The whiteness of Christmas—I see the snowflakes reflected in your eyes. Today is the first snowfall. I see you from the upstairs window. You're down in the yard staring out over the hills into the valley. The people live there and we live up on this hill away from their language and their blistered imaginations. Nobody has visited us in a long time. When you can't die like people you can't really live like them either. This is why we stay here. Above the valley and hidden away. I'm fairly sure you're crying but my vision isn't what it used to be. Part of me thinks about calling to you, but a larger part tells me to keep quiet. I turn another page in the human's notebook and read a bit more of the story that once unwound itself far from our Iceland and in another time.

After that winter I got sick and left in my sleep. You got sick too but they found you lying in the snow and breathing terribly. They couldn't speak our language so they put you in this forgotten corner away from our place. A blue jay nested outside your window and brought me your news. Like a skipped stone, I hoped this dream of us would have the momentum to reach you in time.

From up here we can see the city in its collected brightness. The people and their dreams are pulsating points of light that hum low tones to no one and everyone. A radio washes back and forth through stations somewhere off in the distance. The mountain's edges form a saw-wave on an oscilloscope in a gray Soviet hospital. Our hinterland infirmary is somewhere off a road across powdered landscapes. A woman in her mid-50s sits on the front step and looks out over the sleeping plains. The sky is the color of broken supply lines and slack telephone wires pregnant with dead air. I've come here from other places looking for the person they keep at the end of a long unlit corridor. Beauty slips out from under the door and moves like snakes through the halls trailing cotton bandages and sparkling diamond-cut happiness. The beauty brushes by the woman on the porch like a cat in a dark kitchen somewhere upstate. Right now it's 12:51 AM everywhere. And again, it's not.

Out over the ocean this moment is the only now. Outside of this time there are only Befores that have happened and Befores that will happen. A violent shatterproof beauty skims the waves toward Pitcairn. And here I sit waiting for a passing ship to pick me up at the shore of one of the most isolated places on the planet. Again no sign of you anywhere. It's hard to believe a Cloud made it out this far. This time I thought I'd found you but my clues and guesses got tangled up in the knob-and-tube wiring from our old house. Miro Island spends another night alone. No more passing ships. The Cloud seems to have decided against some of us and moves deeper into uncharted grayness. And your echo bypasses this little island one more time.

Out here there aren't any real clouds. The ocean swims slow laps between continents. Haunted currents pull the light down as far as they can. Not far enough. So deep only silt clouds sewn from tiny particles of decay. The people above know more about Mars than they do about our home. Down here we make our own light. Another unreal sun. Someday I want to visit the world of wind and air and trees and other dry things. For now I'll stay here on the bottom of this ocean trench watching bioluminescent fish dialog in chemical light. From my domed room the creatures and their quivering beacons form an underwater star system of fluid constellations— floating points of self-generated whiteness in a black that stretches farther than everything. I stare out of rounded glass and soon I fall asleep with my head resting on the corner of the table. I dream about a world I know nothing about. I draw a picture of this place in my sleep. It's made from stories that were told in other times by other versions. Out over the fields I see a house and clouds so white they echo a perfect white gold blankness. My feet are stained green and the surface of this world is damp and exploded with thick voices.

A blonde woman appears in one of the windows where her hair ties itself into a golden world of pitch-perfect knots that thickens around the house. A melody played on a glass harmonica pushes itself up from the warm verdant earth. Before long there's a woman standing beside me—a few splatters of blood left dried on her arm. She whispers heady curses into my ear as we listen to the growing tremor of sound and then drown in clouds of her tangled yellow hair. A cloud with less malice. A new species perhaps.

When they first found me I was unconscious. My hair was matted with congealing blood and sea salt. I couldn't speak their language and I had no record or memory of my journey. Now my hair is long and the sun has turned it a paler blonde. I have little recollection of how I came here or why I can communicate with you. Only you.

We are densities. We are movements of narrow bundles. Vibrational emotions. The world is always-only densities. The Office Building. On one of the upper floors the city becomes an unraveling thickness of seas. A shoreline with different boats. I hear a woman who could be you but her voice is the victim of a stickier gravity. And it reverberates wildly. Before long I'm asleep. Now I see myself as I search the rooms of the Office Building—abandoned and full of dust. A ruptured city filled with half-lives. Stray dreams shoot out across space. Snakes chased from the hills in West Virginia. I can see green hills dotted with wildflowers. A house shelters in some pines at the end of a gravel drive. These densities are wrapped in new and gentle ways. In the upstairs window of the painted-white house I see a blonde woman with a windswept smile looking out over the expanse of forgotten dreams and strange fish. I look back at our seaside city. Now there's only a cloudless ocean stretched out like time into forever.

I can't be sure which Before this is but I know I've seen part of it already. Tattered moments hanging in trees. A northern forest pushes the border of a field of yellow flowers—the house and the woman fold into another layer of birch bark static. I'm a visitor lost and found without proper clearance. I wonder how she might stop the flow of blood and time.

It always starts this way and ends in sunflowers. In my memories of this Before I can see her white legs moving between the woody green stalks. One of her socks is slouching its way to the ground. Her left ankle is flecked with watery spring dirt. She walks in navy blue slip-ons with pale yellow embroidery across the top. Dark soil like the color of the bottom of the ocean. On and on through the summer and I'd almost forgotten the smells. I think back to standing beside this woman. Over a sink of unwashed golden beets. Looking out over a million sunflowers that ripple like a Chinese dragon's back as the wind turns their heads in every direction. I look over and follow a narrow river of blood that forms quiet droplets on the beets. She's dying of something we can't find. And now, sunflowers brush my cheeks as I follow her deeper into a sweet and softly rotted summer. A million petaled supernovas in miniature and the rise and fall of humankind. I curve my lives around hers as I follow a path that always leads me back to the edge of the island. And here I am standing like a memory on the shoreline. Always looking out to sea.

Back to another Before with a layer that rises closer to the surface of the sea. Closer to an immanence that holds thicker memories only of you. In this Before you've become a dream. An echo and a dying young woman near the Iowa state line. The car and its headlights sweep along Highway 18 toward Canton. I keep looking over to make sure you're still there. All the lists of our lives, deeply anchored by my glances. I need to make it to Lost Island Lake tonight—I know a pair of Icelandic sisters living there. Maybe they can help. Blacked-out cornstalks on all sides as we drive farther West—one more time and back into the land of the dead.

Some dreams like slivers burrowed in the skin are rotting and slipping their poisoned filigree into our blood. It's a sweet decay like overripe cherries or the summer's expiring infatuations. This is the way I feel about the dreams I've always had of you. In my dreams you speak in languages I can't understand. The snow falls hard on Minnesota today. Out in the yard I see the white outline of winter rushing past like commuters on an imaginary subway. I've never seen a subway in real life. Just in magazines. It's been ages since I've been out of the house. You told me it was too much for me to be out in this weather. You're probably right and a part of me doesn't want to resist. This part is covered by a twenty-five-year-old quilt my mother made for me when I was smaller and less frail. From the window I wonder if you'll come back from the store or if you're gone for good. Maybe you'll just keep driving north past the Twin Cities on through Duluth and up the western shore of Superior and into Canada—never looking back because if you did you'd go deaf from the sound of the winds blowing off the fields and from the roaring emptiness of our house with the pale yellow trim. The border guard asks you how long you intend to stay in Canada. Here you are. You've come back. If we still had a dog she would perk up her ears at the sound of the closing car door. But we don't and you didn't.

I waited in Good Thunder for you to come back, holding a shredded piece of hope. The nail polish grew out and I cut it away without repainting it. I thought about you adrift on some unnamed ocean maybe in a fishing boat. I always think I hear you brushing your teeth upstairs but it's only your ever-hungry echo eating away at my memories. I called you by writing your name in the steam on the bathroom mirror but you were always Away. Maybe you were making another circuit of some vanished island in the North Sea. This is what I'd imagined. Under my breath I swore at my love for you and then I yelled at it and begged it to stop watching me sleep. And then you came back. Almost but not really.

A silence floats near the ceiling. Crying into her face. The paint in this room isn't yellow, it's just faded. The sun picks at the wallpaper like a forty-year scab. She was gone for three years until one day a neighbor found her on her way home from church. She'd taken a different route deviating into the woods to avoid running into an ex-husband she knew would be walking along the main road. The woman found her there lying in musty leaves. The snow-colored skin of her ankles and neck shone in the circles of forest light. She was awake and staring into the branches above her head. When the neighbor approached she sat up and looked through the woman's eyes into a vast Pacific Ocean caught in more dark loops. She turned and followed a path leading back to the old house where she's sitting and looking at the fields across to the woods.

Past the woods and into another Before. A Before only she can see—another lost Soviet heart. This morning there's a new one. The bus coming up from Riga wobbles between rows of wood-burning houses colored bright. There's only one passenger. From another Before. He's searching in reverse, looking for holes in the Berlin Wall and for his father's memory and for his wife and for a museum of horns and antlers—all connected he thinks. Out between the living lodge poles is the country of the Livonians. The logging road takes a bicyclist to the edge of a Before that still lives in the hearts of the last few coastal people. The sound of their voices is almost a fiction now.

This place used to be off limits to foreigners. Up on this Baltic coastline where sand and forests blend, there are streams made by people that lead into wooded endlessness. Other waterways devoured by the laws of perspective. I live along one of these streams in my museum, watching as my tiny music-box garden huddles in the shadows of the pines and the graying sky. I built this museum for you but you never came back. I'm surrounded by birch and filaments of gravel paths and cold-pressed roads that run off to meet an asphalt potential. These roads never hear your voice or the sound of the half-inflated tires of that borrowed bicycle you used to ride. I'm surrounded by thinly sliced dreams and museum things. Now I sleep through most of the winter months.

The museum is in an almost-abandoned seaside village. He has come looking for answers. For all the people who are guided here I keep this museum filled with horns and antlers collected from the woods. For this visitor, I'll open The Library of Other Befores.

I imagine there are unseen areas of the library. Maybe there's a shelf with a book no one has ever wanted or needed close to the floor down several flights of stairs. Maybe this book is where I can find what's been eating you. By now I've been in the library for a few months (I think) looking between pages and rubbed-out lines in the margins. Hunting for answers to questions I don't know how to ask. Encyclopedias of extinct flowers and psychic travel guides and telephone books for towns in countries swallowed up by corruption and ruined economies. An atlas of the Paris catacombs (with several footnotes on echolocation) and a love letter to a dying wife. Forever that.

Farther down the Livonian Coast in the fishing village of Mazirbe there was a house where the previous Librarian had lived before World War II. He'd fallen ill there and could no longer make the daily bicycle trip to the Library. It didn't matter because nobody had needed information about any other Befores in years and the Library had been silent for a long time. One day looking for some fresh salted air I took a ride along the coast in a fishing boat. I knew it would pass by the old Librarian's house in Mazirbe so I'd made arrangements for a pick-up early in the morning. On my lap a threadbare book with the number four written in thick black ink on its water-buckled front page. After a while we rounded a small island and the house came into view. The boat skimmed up on the beach and I jumped out. As the two fishermen headed back out to sea I hoped they really would stop to pick me up on their return trip. I'd been told no one had lived in the house for almost thirty years but I'd been given a key by the current Librarian along with permission to let myself in. The Librarian told me there wasn't much left to see but I was welcome to have a look around. Hungry for the outside some lonesome memories pushed past me as I opened the door. My feet swept away a tiny cordillera of mounded sand on the threshold as I stepped into the house for the first time in many long times.

Book Number Four contained descriptions of all the hallways in the house. Locations along the walls where fissures in the dusty wallpaper had exposed bits of writing. Under yellowy paste and paper the corridors were covered with words and sentences. Chapters and slivers of half-finished novellas. He'd pasted them up during the long Livonian winter as his health steadily declined. He'd worked in bulletproof dedication cutting and gluing his crumbling body sloping closer to the floor every evening. Luckily in the days and years after her husband's death she'd cataloged the writings and their intentions in a book of her own. A kind of instruction manual for reading the house's layered narrative. Soon she died and the new owners re-papered the underwritten walls.

Views To Miro Island: a novel in seventeen parts by F. Noonan

Chapter I – Arrivals and Departures

The sand drifted around my body as I lay beside the folded bits of our plane. Blood caked over my left eye and my lashes stuck together in little red-brown spires. About ten feet away, I saw your hand at the edge of a dune. I immediately tried to stand, but my legs were badly injured. At the other end of the beach, I thought I heard voices through the wind speaking a language I could not place. After a few minutes, I began to make out figures and the balls of light that hung from long poles. Soon they were upon me, lifting me up and into a deep rowboat. I tried to yell out for you, but blood and the sound of waves pushed my voice away, into some other ocean.

From the Latvian house I can see Gimli, Manitoba and past that the dirt road leads off Highway 68 to the hamlet of Reykjavik—a skull of a place picked clean by sunlight and ravens. In one Before (not mine) this place was home to murderers who'd cut themselves into farmers. Lonely Lake calls me with the wild guts of a northern light. The summer nights grow long like bulrushes here and the people are known for their dancing. I can see their dances from across the Baltic. The windows of the house are an orangey green that confuses the moon. From this Before in Reykjavik, Manitoba I hear the story of Orn. Another part of this strange little saga.

On the prairie in the newly formed dawn I saw the lake of grass move apart. An opening with an animal resting low in its entrance. Down to the Earth's insides. Down into the winding burrow past roots and moles. Deeper and following the creature under and across the plain. When the tunnel ended I was standing beside the badger at the edge of a narrow river. And then in one human moment he was gone. Strands of metallic light vibrated. A warm tone from the surface of the water. Comforted by the ambient temperature and gentle noise I fell asleep and floated out into the always-night of the underground. I am Orn of the Western Lands, Land of the Dead, New Iceland.

Orn's Before becomes her before. He slips into her pulse at the ATM. He comes from the after-before back to her in the space underneath her fingernails. He forms a new duty—his debt to be paid. From this waterway to her instep he helps to move her across cold white nights and wild neon glimmer.

In and out of their buildings and cars. People's dreams trailing after them like invisible pets. The dreams unravel and pieces sometimes crack off. I'm this woman's heart. I see out of her left eye all that happens around her. I'm the accumulation of her beauty and ugliness. Her breathlessness and tears and her diamonds and coal. When I see these dream trails I can direct the woman's thoughts to follow other people's dreams. And this is what I do. And my being-Orn arches deeper into her bloodstream.

From this place I fall back through the ground and into another Before. The Icelander is gone and so is the woman. I'm holding a tiny book with a cover that's aged like the leather of cracked cowboy boots. I'm holding your wrist as you start to turn on your snowshoes. Back into the forest.

The snow that has finally come to upstate New York reflects our streetlight making your lacy breath visible along the Hudson's December darkening. Water vapor from your mouth like gray foxes quickening through the trees and across fields at night. Up into the blue-black nothing I follow your fox trails until they disappear into the stars. One more skip traced in pencil.

In another very recent Before she was called A.

. . . and across the ocean to this little island you can't see on your maps.

The way I love you makes my teeth hurt. Snow-blindness and I fall headfirst into another winter and the wind against my face in heavy curls. Now I can sense it again. In this place Befores are always tangled and covered in thick coatings of northern light. As all the things that happened collide at night the ground gives way and then I'm gone again. In loops of time that always try to keep us apart. We were so close—the tundra burned cold and quiet all around us. Across this Siberian plain there are reverberations of another Before that I can't quite touch. Thick like history. There aren't any sounds when the storm passes and I can see a few drops of new blood on the snow. I have to go back to another Before. And I'm in a train car watching the taiga tick by on my way south. Eventually to the Black Sea and then somehow to the oceans.

Views Toward Miro Island

    Chapter XII

    Now I'm back where we began this trip so many years ago, back inside and full of artifice and addiction. I looked for you for so long, my eyes burned-out by tears. I retraced our map, looking for your body a thousand times. Still, at night, and in the wheat fields of the Dakotas, I feel you next to me and you speak softly in their language. Did you forget our English? Do you remember me? How can I take you back from this illness? Where should I find you?

In all the Befores that led us here we tore holes in the paper screens of our histories looking for answers to your death. I can feel head-splitting dreams and postcards in our hands as I tug your Before deeper into my infected woods.

Before this Before we made our lives on an unnamed island in a southern ocean. Our sailboat struck land at night. We found an abandoned house with a pool. We kept ourselves alive by growing a few vegetables from salvaged seeds and catching strange fish. The sun played an invisible piano somewhere down at the end of the beach. The house had over thirty rooms but we only used a few of them. Rooms filled with papers and dust. Often the windows were no more than lines of light at the top of the wall. We spent some of our days sifting through pages and looking for words we could understand. All the stories of other Wyomings and other Befores were written in cryptic looping cursive. Some of the stories disintegrated in our hands. Maps of unknown Wyomings sometimes surfaced on the crest of paper waves before folding back into themselves—a United States of Wyomings: perfectly square. I started to piece together related Befores but then I found the collection of writings about music boxes in one of the many orange-red cabinets.

The sun falls behind the horizon. White gold again. The smell of seawater and sunlight thickens in my blood. I desperately want to turn back to the house and run across the lawn past the blue pool house through the kitchen and up the back stairs. At the top I imagine I'll catch you falling. Your weight is diamond-hard—your limbs tight. Wild saplings tethered. Your last breath is an errant note from a broken harp frozen as it moves across the Pole. I want to run back but I stay silent and still at the edge of our island. As long as I'm here you'll still be alive and your disease will sleep one more night. The wind picks up and the sun has gone. When it's darker I walk back up the dock to the house. I wonder if you're asleep at the top of the stairs.

Instead of waking you I lie down on the worn-out carpet to quietly touch my head to yours. As I dream another Before that's so close to this one branches from my forehead spin dark lines in a retelling of a set of stories. To briar our heads together. This one takes place in summer and there are other people in the trees.

The woods are quieter tonight. The brightest stars through branches overhead. The moon's light rests up against the trees leaning like a tired dream. There are other people here with us in autumn's unsound. I can see you half-remember me by the way your eyes follow mine. Even in the dark. We're gathered here in the forest at the edge of a field waiting for the thing that brought us here. A cure at the end of a path that only appears once every twenty-five years. A break from the loops and Clouds. An erasure of broken circles. We wait for a space to open in the underbrush. An alligator moves soundlessly through the tangled microcosm—then a faint clear melody in the air. A music box.

Two Befores converge in Iowa on two sisters living beside a lake.

Out on the bridge across our lake I lie with my face against these tired boards. My hair loops down in small rings of only a few strands. On the surface of the lake, we heard the sound and saw the pine tree pushing out above the leaves. A street made of alligator backs winds past our place and sinks quietly like old-time letters into the forest on the other side of the lake. Another Before across the same water.

The sister has gone Away and days fall like tamarack needles in autumn—layered and crossed. She packed her suitcases and walked the seven miles to the train station to catch a ride to the airport. A plane took her Away. A freshly abandoned island with an empty house. Curtained floors and a thick dark cellar. Her plane crashed but she survived alone on the western face of this blood clot of land. The house is too quiet—she sleeps on the beach beside one of the washed-up pontoons.

Now my hands make photographs by framing the events of our life in willful little rectangles. I draw invisible edges in the wind trying to memorize their contents. My mind holds countless rows of filing cabinets full of these pictures. Under the whispered first-floorboards there are other spaces. My memory-photos are incomplete. Many only have three sides. Remembrances seep out and swim across the dark basement gurgling in off-color eddies and recollections. Half of her lipstick and a filament of cloud-light and three notes from a Bulgarian Easter hymn. The end of a sentence spoken in anger and sadness. Sand accumulates around me as I sleep on the beach dreaming of hands and pictures and trying to put the shards of my life together at the edge of the ocean on maybe the most distant shore in this world.

Some other Before—one that wasn't written in towers of paper—once played out on this island. There were two families living here. Each side of the island was the province of one family. A deep canyon sawed through the island's middle. Instead of face-to-face interactions the families wrote letters to each other sending them through the forest on a preexistent rope-and-pulley system. The notes moved along the line in small glass jars. One father studied the strange fish in the unknown sea that surrounded the island. The mother on the other side of the island studied the migration patterns of human dreams. The kind of fish that didn't want to be known to people lived in the island's waters. It was also a popular resting place for dreams on their nightly journeys from head to head. They nested there in the thousands. Later in the life of the island and in the life of the people the fish and dreams became less numerous, and eventually there were only a few fish and dreams left to study. The dreams that did arrive on the island were disjointed and clouded and the fish became sad and gray swimming in careless circles. The final note came from one side to the other: "An elevator in our house will take us back tomorrow. You really can't be late."

I think the answer I've been looking for in all of these Befores lives in the faded dreams and infrequent fish of this nameless island at the edge of the world. The story wasn't written, it was told to me in a dream. In this Before, I wake up in the clipped silence of a forlorn wing of this house. Four in the morning—I hear a cockroach rummaging in a tin can on the kitchen counter. I fall back into a kind of sleep. I dreamt about the space between a summer dress and your skin. The temperature and humidity are perfect in this little microclimate. It is a placeless space that tells circled stories about my infatuation.

We're on the beach beside an old wide lake. Under a lime tree with only a few fruits left on it you made promises your body couldn't keep. Your skin is healthy and smothered with sun. A small vein of sadness runs down my arm. I know this can't last.

The house sits empty now. No people, only faint shadows and distant jars filled with festering peaches and moldy summer cherries. The gentle death of fruit floats above our heads where honeybees and crows remain. There are no shades to lower—they're already packed away. Just as well. The afternoon sun spilling through the windows softens my mournfulness for a minute. Out in the wheat I see that familiar image of you. You're in a blue-and-white-checkered dress holding a straw hat against your leg. Looking Away your movements compliment the yellow grain and ocean-colored cotton. The sky goes on into another forever and you walk steadily Away until you're out of view. I stand on the veranda with a cardboard box of your things. The day moves into night and the stars quietly remind themselves to constellate. The North Star pulls both of us through evening: me in my dying car, you along the silent strings of a summer night's wind.

The wind pushes birdsongs in through the sunroof as I drive away from the swaying desert and your cotton mouthed kiss. And then I'm beside a road in Serbia in May in a Before that seems to burn brighter than the others. Hot with blood memories. A violent magnetism grabs me and I push the little car through the evening tree branches on an isolated mountain road. And then I'm lying on the beach beside the same broken airplane but your hand is nowhere.

Birdsongs form a new grammar out of leaves. The notes echo in the wind as I follow them down through the trees. Always into the darker parts of the woods to stands of pine I've never seen. It's getting late now and Serbia's campfire stories wrap themselves around me. Always tighter with a warm blackness. The last lips and teeth of daylight skitter across the stream as I cross into an audience of trees. The sound of my footsteps turns pillowy as the sun gets sucked into the oily night. There can be no reversing, no change of hearts. I feel something that reminds me of the birdsongs but it sounds and feels nothing like them. And now there are people on either side of me. Two. I can't see them but I feel the heat of their touch. Slowly light pushes its way into the forest and moves toward us. Cement and broken-out windows and a tall dead building in front of the moon. At the edge of the woods Bergen's valley bites down and I'm taken to another Wyoming leaving these smoldering bandages behind.

Inside the building there's a suburban house in Massachusetts. As I step through the doorway Serbia bleeds away into printed words. Befores cluster around me like blackberry seeds—a few are rotten some drip overripe in a Cape Ann summer. I think back to how I got here. Another Before makes itself into a drawing in a book in a dream I had in another Before. When I wake up I'm back in the Serbian forest, standing beside my wrecked rental car with its headlights pointing in different directions as their beams slice at the half-real night. And I'm following the sounds of water droplets into the darkness.

Trees edge the street as linear and uniform as the houses they shade. I follow the same path every day. I see worn-thin women in their puffed-out houses. Bay windows and French doors. Pools like backyard lakes and today their water is still like their northern cousins. Winter huddles up against the end of the month and the children having become marginally adult are off at their northeastern colleges. A distracted autumn paws the ground and the soundless sky half-heartedly thinks about rain. In my driveway and the car stops. I stare for a moment at the almost colorless paint on the garage before I step out of the car and into the steppe. I fall about three feet into an Outer Mongolia. I see you off in the distance. Your toes holding the rocky ledge as you balance yourself over your feet like a carefully perched snowy owl. Your pale blue dress whips wildly around your knees in the powdery desert light. We're gone in an instant and I find you lying in a pool of sun in the back room. Vermont's October finds resting places in the curve of you left ear. You are even more bird wings now.

A snowy owl. A Russian daughter.

The snow shifts itself into light. Tonight the whole world hides under a dark blue quilt with a lamp shining warmly on the other side. You're sleeping. I look out the bedroom window and up the street as it fills with snow. Our room is lit with weird light and the whiteness falls so quietly it's almost deafening. Your breaths alternate between labor and rest. Some are filled with pops and scratches like an old record and others are smooth like a new beach. You're dying out as you sleep and here I stand, face against the cold winter glass, thinking about your twenty-year-old cheeks in the photo from a summer cabin up north. I'm careful to draw out all of our moments as far as possible.

I think back to a prewritten Before. One that bends back on the Befores we've already known. In this Before you're an old friend from school lost to me for decades. Only cryptic telegrams and bland postcards from Wisconsin. I found you here beside yourself along a cold rocky lakeshore. You were dying. Before you died we boarded the plane and later that week we were shading our foreheads from the French-African sun and its reflection on the ocean.

Before we left for the island there were parts of your house I'd never seen, words I'd never heard in your mouth. In the pre-morning light of the one-bedroom apartment where you used to live I saw crumpled dreams lying on the floor next to your salt-stained sneakers. Soon you'll know your own magnitude. We're standing on an island named after you somewhere out in one of our nameless oceans. The winds play old punk records in your ears and the cupped seashells tell you you're home.

Befores move in and out so quickly now. Their arrivals and departures become increasingly unpredictable. This place can't be too far from the edge of the world. I'm pulled into the closer Before that ties me to you and our search and the island and the dreams and dying. We're beside a river and you're kneeling, dark flecks of dirt pinpointing your feet. Black rock under snowy Japanese and/or Icelandic landscapes. I catch the smell of your hair as it winds its way through the humidity and leaves. I remember these Befores not like they were my own. It's as if your Befores were sent to me on this island in a dream. I see myself but it's not my Self, it's someone else with my teeth. They tumble on broken wings. The paintbrush origin of always more Wyomings drifting out of control. I'm awake in a bed on Miro. The morning is cloudless and quiet with a bloodless certainty. Today I asked someone in the village on the western shore if there would be any boats coming by in the next few weeks. He looked confused. All the maps I've found on this island have been uniformly incomplete with the strange exception of a map of Wyoming that hangs in the tiny harbor bar. I trace the topographic outlines of the Great Divide Basin while I drink burned-out rum and stare across the cleanly emptied cove.

Along the stream in another Before a hundred autumn colors rip themselves open splilling red-gold blood on your face. Sunlight catches your shoulders. Your dream is dense and pulpy. The tones of light saturate to forever and voices vibrate at odd frequencies. Your dreams are always poisonously beautiful. They always lead us back to the island. It's such a wild never. An emerald prison.

Once I caught one of your dreams—just a tiny piece, a pottery shard. It flickered and flitted on my palm for a moment and then evaporated into the city's night. You were beautiful like fire in that miniature cloud that evening beside my pillow. And now our heads and dreams are so far apart. The wind blows hard out of Muddy Gap tonight and the locket with a little piece of your inside, swings from my car's rear view mirror as I roll past the Bairoil turn-off and deeper into the Basin.

In a motel room in Jeffrey City I found another notebook—only one page had anything written on it.

Things not to forget in other Befores:

    1. Snow in Vermont

    2. JWA 1949

    3. Miro Island (have to find coordinates and leave them behind for him)

    4. Highway 18 (2 miles past Orkney)

    5. Possible routes through this Wyoming (is this the last one? Is it his?)

    6. Owls and woodchucks

    7. 17 Befores remaining

We climbed the steep dusty road past departed miner's homes locked-out on the edge of the hills. We walked on into dense leaves and wiry branches that whisper-whipped our backs. The remnants and revenants that live in these houses are too poor to repaint and their televisions and Bibles are forever misplaced. Some of the shadows here are made out of people who still live but they've been eaten by the cities and mini-malls at the edge of the capital. The person we're looking for lives deep in these woods so warm and dark filled with so many moths and possums.

In the book I carry there are familiar words and others that aren't even made of human language. It's from a Before that hasn't happened yet. There's a map drawn in blue ballpoint pen near the back of the book and I recognize some of the names of towns from my childhood. And here we are, you and I, at the edge of this clearing in the woods. She steps out into the half night. She's the last of her kind so far from Iceland here in these strange hills. The last hidden person on Earth warms her words in her mouth and speaks them. Sparrows rushing out of an old barn. Her hair is silver but she still seems much younger than you or I. Her words come to rest in the trees and slowly they fall into sentences. She draws you up against her chest and whispers a lonely valley in Norway. Maybe this will be the last Before.

These are the first few lines of the book I carry:

And wiley care do next the shatter of cabots on the Worley trail under flashing night that glasses thraming with glimonning specters. No more the cause of our dire and golm mither. Take from this place a frontical of treeminas and place hef lock a purl ofle that glory now upon the shadows.

This was the last Before I would know. I can only watch you from Away while you start to unimagine me. The Clouds are almost everywhere. Even out to the island. You can't ever truly forget me but in your head my image begins to unwind and fray into the winter night following the cottage warmth in smoke signals for nebulas.

In what I think is my last Before, I'm written like an echo. I'm written to wander in loops of forested light on invisible feet. I remember being alive and I think I must have been happy. I miss you and your humanness. I miss the sound of your hair moving through hairbrush teeth. Sometimes I hover at the edge of these woods trying to breathe in stray bits of real clouds. I look out along the fields and past other forests to where you might still live. Without me. I spend some of my time playing dominoes with the badger. Our game pieces are chunks of bark. He's gnawed out the lines and dots. I visit the old fox in the western corner of the bramble thicket at least once a week. He tells me stories of being human. Of dying. I tell him the same stories. The crows paint fissured noise with their darkness and I'm still thinking and dreaming through a wooded imagination. Out in your world the animals are quiet. Here they're the world's memories cast in fur and claws. I'm only points in space moving along directionless desire lines.

In a shivering stand of birch. Now an echo dreams all the Befores and all the never-Befores. Lying purposeful and quiet beside a stream coveted by moonlight.

All of these ghost stories are already written. Picking fireweed along the dreams that cross Saskatchewan and South Dakota I find a few loose threads from your skirt. The wind double-backs to crumple my words. In a prairie Before we sit at the top of our rolled-out hill looking down into the half-valley and the dried-up riverbed. Small blood-lettings slip from the corner of your mouth. You pretend not to notice because you think it'll ruin our fading summer happiness. I let it drip. You're getting sicker and parts of our dreams are starting to get worn-out in certain corners. Dog-eared memory. Where the seams meet the spaces are ever widening. Your arms are thinner now and I worry they'll get lost in the corn stalks. I hold you tight and breathe in the High Plains air that rests like dust on your skin. Then the sun is gone and we're left without shadows. The stars collect the sky and crows turn transparent. You lay your head in the bend of my arm and fall asleep. Down in the valley there's a man who once hosted a half-famous talk show. His looping fingerprints are maps for making you better. Always more lines for us to follow. But we've walked so far tonight on this alligator road and the nights are still warm enough to sleep outside. In the morning we'll follow the curve of the hills to the valley floor. Sleep covers us in a quilt made of fresh blue jeans and scuffed-up plastic jewels. Fireweed burns a fever onto my dreams. By now you've forgotten our language. My words are only a disenchanted mist. And the once-deep cut healed itself long ago.

As we sleep, our dreams pass each other as pieces of a shipwreck floating in an Indian Ocean. I wonder from inside my sleep if our Befores can be lived through in dreams. I reach into the water trying to pull some of your smaller dreams closer but they're still alive—squirming out of my hands like thick dark eels. My dreams are hollow and see-through and they drift away soundlessly into another night. Your night. In the lamplight caught in the fold of a sail I watch a Before unravel itself along echoing hills of waves. Of wheat.

Your dreams sometimes form themselves into folded paper boats—hundreds of them fill our bedroom. Most are pink but there are a few blue ones. Some are pale orange. When I unfold one little particles of light roll out onto the floor and scurry under the bed: the sound of electric parakeets. Mostly I leave the dream-boats alone. I brush them aside with my feet as they navigate between old cats and solitary socks. Today one of your dreams lingers in the corner of the room. It starts to grow. And now I'm inside a dream cloud and our bedroom is gone. Sounds from a music box and bent tree roots and leaves share the edges of the trail. Lights made by insects lead off the path to a door covered with Portuguese ceramic tiles. In one of the upper windows the otter presses his furry face against the glass and now I'm in another room where the folded paper boats are for sale. They're meticulously cataloged and categorized by shape and date and rarity of color.

He agrees to sell me an orange boat and I sit down to read the newly unfolded dream. It's about a newly married couple. So in love. In this dream there are other, smaller dreams so I'll have to watch this one carefully so it doesn't get lost. It'll show me the trails through the forest that lead me home. For now this dream is a map, a journey from a haunted death.

Outside our room another wind infects the night. Blue pushes against deep black. Out there in the car we can sit together in loneliness, pulsating through the interstates. In another Before, you're asleep. Into rattlesnake country and we pass the memories of adobe houses in the hills. A hauntedness covered in skin and denim. Earlier that day we stopped to eat at a restaurant off the I-90 where you met the woman who would find us on the side of the road later that night.

Farther on, we rest the car in roadside lots with bathrooms and pop machines. When you come out of the stall you find the woman powdering her forehead. As you wash your hands you catch her eye in a corner. Instantly you're gone across wintered slopes and it's three hundred years ago out into another Before. She tugs at your sleepy arms dragging you through wild snow-fields. In another Before I'm waiting for you to come back to the car. The interior lights are on and I'm talking without much interest to a kid driving to New York from Washington. I keep wondering about you but I remember and know Befores are all relative and you might be right beside me slipping in and out of the car's light or the reflection of the moon on the hood.

In this woman's Before portraits with small eyes and thick white wigs cluster in dark hallways. We left footprints in the falling snow as we clipped noiselessly toward the inside-glow of the house on the hill. I wondered if you were still waiting for me beside the car. Our hems moved across crystal-flakes of unknown variation. My hand is circumscribed by hers and the hurtful red of her nails quietly scratches my wrist. The sleigh waits at the edge of the field and the horses with their bobbed tails scrape at the frozen dirt. She pulls me along beside her as the plumpness of her whiteness and affluence pulps over her every edge. Her hair hangs like strings of gaslit sugar and spears off into the night. Trundling and tumbling we dash up the stairs that clap against our slippers. And now we're inside spirits evaporating in our pink breath. This place is empty and filled with looping specters. This is the House of Befores and we are its sister-keepers. The Dreamers and their Clouds cannot enter this place. In our tattered imagination we slump into mothy chairs and uncurl our languages with hot irons until they look like people. Off into the blistered evening the sleigh and its horse. We drown ourselves in chalky powder and fermented apathy.

And while you sleep away the Before where you're less sick I'm playing music on a pump organ. I'm a part of a story about a father and son and a thin line of affection that weaves itself into dreamcatchers and straw hats. Wyoming blooms full tilt in the early morning light as we follow our paths back to the beginning. I rest in certainty tonight knowing that in your Before you are alive and the roundness has returned to your face. She keeps you safe tonight in the snowy hills in abandoned houses on islands at the edge of the world.

Parts of my native Before are underwater now. The northern places are wooded and full of tin-roofed houses and straight scaly pines. In the south the wind and ice persuade our tires into restful roadside eateries. When I was younger I'd sit in the swirl of the dust with my father, in an old truck that sometimes picked up hitchhikers on the road to the dump. On these prairies people used to live in houses made out of dirt. We live in a house cut from gray wood. Falling silently to ruin. I rest my head against your young-father arm. The back seat is filled with sunlight and shards of colored glass. Now we're on the other side of the border and I'm almost thirty. The car is newer but still old and we drive into the night where stars and snow bleed into one another. Fragments of dreams embed themselves in our skins. I ask my father if he wants to listen to *Graceland* again but he's asleep. On into the night that holds my hand with a willowy grip.

I know this is the place. The pages from all the books in all the Befores led me here. All the openings to other times carefully mapped and the calculations transcribed into specific points. These locations. I feel your arms around my neck and I see the old leopard walk across the highway into a cornfield. I pull the car over and run out into the night after his shadow. Green leaves and stalks punch at my shins and forearms as I rush to catch the middle of all of the Befores that we've ever and never been. Dizzy and disjointed I fall into the Minnesota darknesses. When I open my eyes we're walking on a trail through the New Mexico hills near Colonias. It must be about four in the morning.

We've come to the end of this path. Night falls into day as we continue through the hills. We keep climbing into the heat of afternoon. I've come here to lay you among the rust-colored stones and broken sunlight. We stop to rest and I press my cheek against your eye sockets. A small low breath seeps from your Nebraska-born mouth. Under a small outcrop we lay together and you fade into nothing and I fall into your open silhouette. Now we're weightless gripping each other's hands so tightly. Into a meadow with a big white house at the far end. We can see a lawn and a pool house and columns of steps leading up to the front door. Lifted on a wave of prairie grasses our footsteps become vanished echoes. I kiss you to feel your face against my old world cheek one more time. You're safe forever and now we're dead together. I wake up beside you in the white house.

Views Toward Miro Island
       Chapter XVII

       A series of music boxes lined up on the windowsill of our bedroom. Each is labeled with the name of a Before that might bring me back to you, in time for us to end this book together, forever. I've worked on the formulas and equations, the sequences and notes, and today is the day I perform my piece and bring all of our Befores together into a shining Now. All of our language will be gone and there won't be any more books or highways. There will be no here or there, and Miro Island and the deepness of rowboats will be gone forever. Today, I'll kiss you in nothingness and always. I can only love you.

In your face in that final moment I see the paths and loops that brought us here. I see the Icelandic sisters and their pet owl in their wintery house on an island. There are memories of badgers and otters and cats and crows and foxes and groundhogs all along the edges of your smile. I still don't understand some of the words you speak in your sleep. There are faint scars on your legs and you're always wearing that pair of aviator goggles around your neck. Every so often up here in our own little Wyoming I find you laying against a rock or beside a stream speaking into the dirt in a strange language. Tonight we'll lie in the grass and remember the other Befores and the way we looked back then holding hands as tight as we can until we fall asleep under our secret Wyoming sky. Sleep well tonight my golden cousins. No more Befores. This is the end of our wayfaring. We are still holding hands as night washes us away and over the powdered outline of another shattered Wyoming. I lean a little closer and let your hair blow across my face. Out in the prairie midnight at last. I love you always now painlessly and endlessly. Forever Now.

EPILOGUE 1

48°17'36.55"N, 89°47'51.71"W
50°27'25.81"N, 105°49'6.32"W
47°17'38.82"N, 91°16'45.53"W
44°28'33.52"N, 73°12'39.43"W
44°51'37.50"N, 58°55'48.65"W
48°10'50.79"N, 99°48'3.45"W
65°42'39.71"N, 21°41'55.20"W
51°50'27.02"N, 107°36'29.13"E
42°29'41.29"N, 107°49'38.83"W
53°10'24.96"N, 107°39'45.00"E
46°51'44.99"N, 103°50'47.96"E
25° 3'58.39"S, 130° 6'9.75"W
43°43'35.88"N, 101°58'47.34"W
42°26'40.51"N, 76°29'57.33"W
35° 6'34.49"N, 104°50'45.70"W
55°49'43.05"N, 37°38'1.13"E
24°21'41.27"S, 128°18'58.95"W

A river of white fish
Horizons and dugouts
An iron hole in the night
One of our first houses
Owl's other home
See-through houses and an opening to Miro
Sister-keepers
Prayer flags and a girl's hair unwound
Another notebook, mostly empty
As seen from the edge of North Dakota by an old leopard
Three feet below another before
The crash
Bad land
An abandoned cat
Badger's hills
ВДНХ
Portia wood without clocks

EPILOGUE 2

Justin Armstrong was born in Moose Jaw, Saskatchewan and grew up in the woods near Thunder Bay, Ontario. He teaches writing and anthropology at Wellesley College and lives in Boston with his wife, Heather and their dog, Trout.